Python's Party

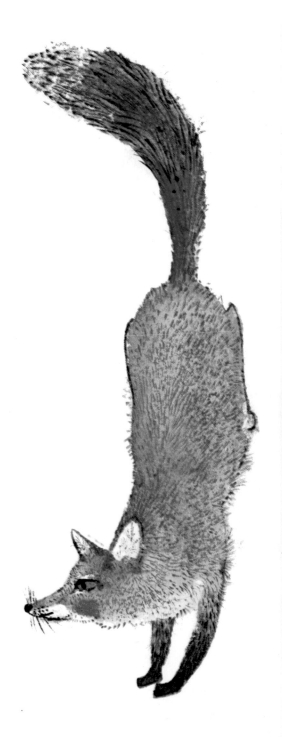

FOR AURELIE

All rights reserved.
First published 1974 by Oxford University Press, London.
First American publication by Franklin Watts, Inc., New York, 1975.
SBN: 531-02808-9
Library of Congress Catalog Card Number: 74-20303
5 4 3 2 1

Printed in U.S.A.

FRANKLIN WATTS, INC.
NEW YORK, N.Y. 1975

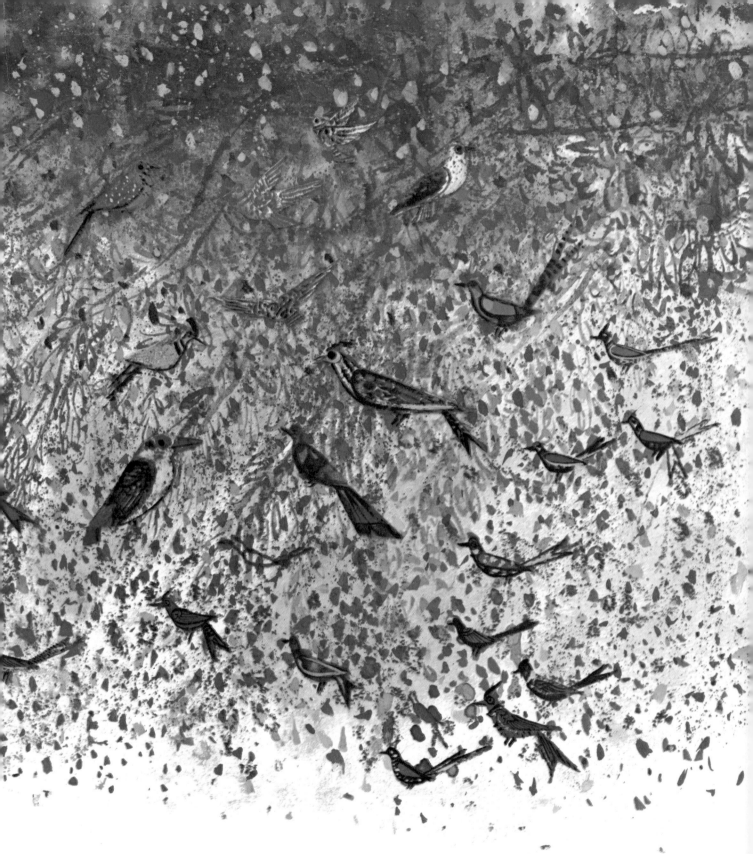

Python's Party

BRIAN WILDSMITH

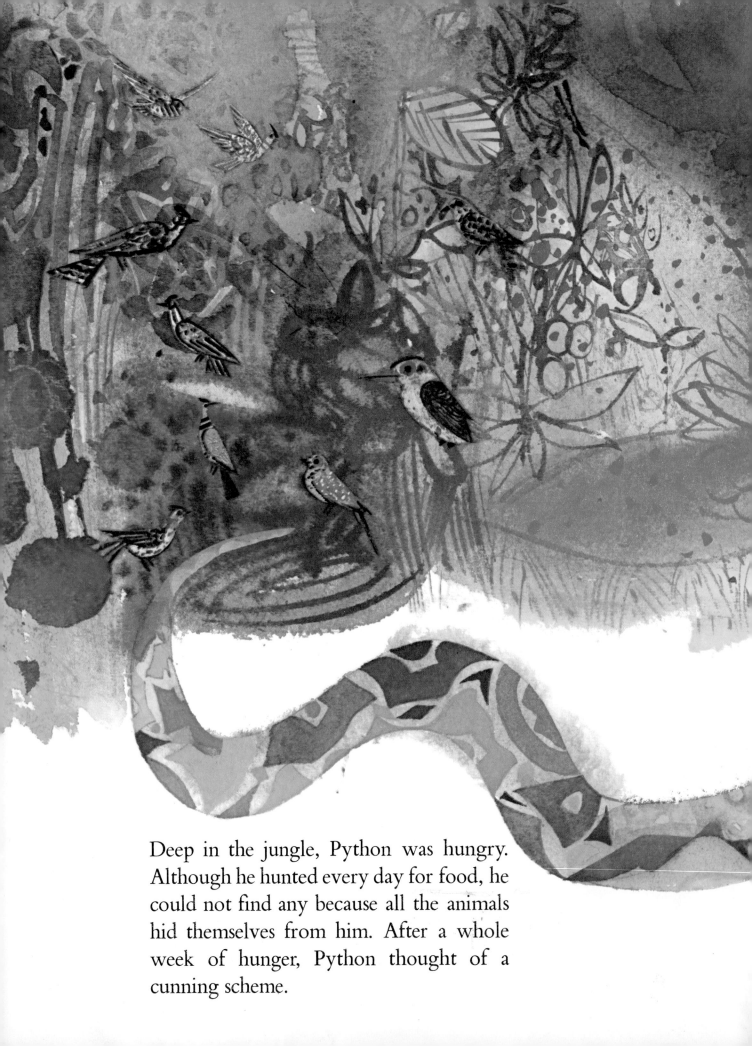

Deep in the jungle, Python was hungry. Although he hunted every day for food, he could not find any because all the animals hid themselves from him. After a whole week of hunger, Python thought of a cunning scheme.

He climbed a tall tree, and called out in a loud voice: "Friends, I know you are hiding from me, but don't be afraid. I promise to be good, and to show you that I mean it, I invite you all to my party."

Several animals crept near to the tree to listen—though they all felt nervous and were ready to run if Python started to come down.

Zebra and Parrot muttered that they did not believe Python could be good, but Python heard them and called down again. "On my honor, I promise to behave myself. Everyone will be safe at my party."

Goat and Fox thought they ought to believe him, and anyway they liked parties. So they persuaded the others, and everyone

accepted Python's invitation. Python slithered down the tree like lightning, full of ideas for the party.

"Let's have a competition to see who can do the cleverest tricks," he shouted, and everyone thought it a great idea. "I'll be master of ceremonies," cried Parrot, "and announce what each one is going to do."

So the animals sat down and thought hard about the tricks that they would perform, and when they were ready Parrot went around so that they could whisper in his ear.

Then the party began. Parrot cried out:
"The first trick is to be given by Gnu and Jungle Fowl, with a little help from Chameleon."

The audience watched, and shouted, "Not bad.
Not bad." And clapped as loud as they could.

"And now for a feat never before seen in this forest. The world-famous Hyena will walk on two round melons for a distance of twenty yards!"
The audience were very impressed, and held their breath while Hyena wobbled along.

"That's great," they said. "That trick will be hard to beat."

"Now for an act of strength and balance by none other than the spotted Leopard and four agile Monkeys."

"Wow!" said the audience. "These tricks get better and better."

"Quiet now for my lord Lion," cried Parrot.
Lion, who had been behind some bushes dabbing himself with mud, now stepped proudly forward, and looked at them all.
"You can have three guesses at what I am supposed to be," he said.
"A lion pretending to be a leopard."

"No," sniffed Lion.

"A domino!"

Lion looked puzzled, and shook his head. He had never heard of a domino before.

"A lion with dirt on him," called out a baby guinea fowl.

Lion roared with laughter. "No. I am a lion with measles!"

"Now for a double act," Parrot put in quickly, because he thought the audience looked rather huffed. "Fox and Genet will now entertain us."
The audience cheered up and clapped and stamped their feet.
"Good, good," they shouted.

Parrot forgot what Zebra was going to do, but Zebra did not wait to be announced anyway. He balanced coconuts on his back hoofs, threw them up in the air, and as they came down, kicked them into little pieces.

"That's wonderful," the audience cried and scuffled about excitedly.

Parrot was nearly as excited as the audience, and he rather muddled up his announcement of the last act.

"Our fine feathered friend, Pelican, will endeavor to collect as many fine feathered friends—I mean, as many friends—with or

without feathers—as many friends as possible into his beak."
Pelican had fixed it up beforehand with some members of the
audience and they rushed out to climb into his capacious mouth.
"My word," the rest of the animals breathed, in awe. "That really
takes some beating."

Python stretched himself and smiled.

"Oh, I don't know," he said modestly. "I believe I can do better than that. I could get more of you into my mouth than the Pelican."

By this time everyone was too excited to be cautious.

"All right," they said. "If you think so, you have a try."

So Python opened his mouth wide, and they all began to climb into it. Soon some of them decided that they didn't like it inside Python. "All right, you win," they called out from one end of Python to the other. "It's dark in here and we would like to come out now." Python closed his mouth with a snap.

"I'm sorry," he said, in a hissing voice. "But now that I have you, I mean to keep you. I have been hungry for long enough."

When they realized they had been tricked, the animals began to shout and bang about, but Python was not disturbed and lay down to enjoy a gentle snooze. He had no sooner dropped off than Elephant came by, and heard the shouting coming from the sleeping snake. He walked across to see what was happening, and the animals knew it was he by his heavy tread.

"Elephant, Python has tricked us and we are all shut up inside here and can't get out," they called, in muffled and tearful voices. Elephant did not waste words.

Instead, he lifted up his foot and stamped hard on Python's tail.

Python woke up with a start, and opened
his mouth with a shout of pain.

Immediately the animals began to tumble
out as fast as possible, and Elephant kept

his foot firmly on Python's tail until the
last one had escaped.

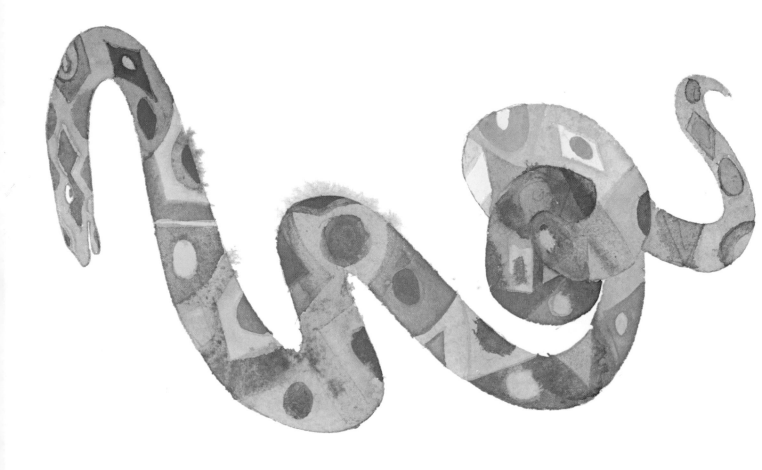

"That was a very nasty trick," the animals told Python.
And while Elephant stood guard, they tied a knot in
Python's tail. "That is to remind you," they said severely,
"not to do it again." "And let it remind you, too," Elephant
said to the animals, "never to play with Python, even at
his own party."
But the animals said they wouldn't need a knot to remind
them never again to go to a party given by a python.